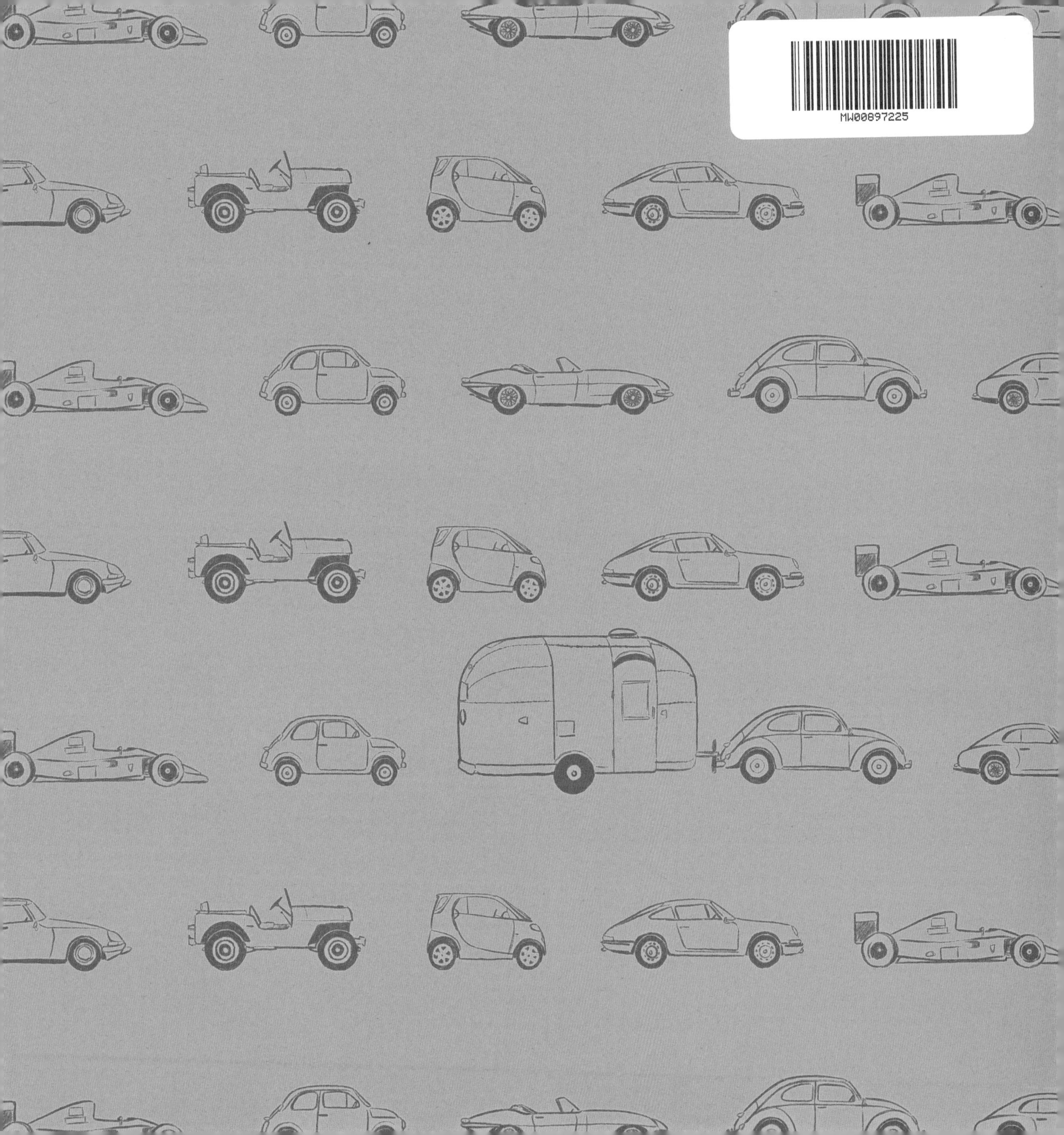
MW00897225

For August, who I'm sure will one day make the car of his dreams—*K. W.*

Published in conjunction with the exhibition
Automania, at The Museum of Modern Art, New York,
July 4, 2021–January 2, 2022

Allianz

***Automania* is made possible by Allianz,
MoMA's partner for design and innovation.**

Produced by the Department of Publications
The Museum of Modern Art, New York

Hannah Kim, Business and Marketing Director
Don McMahon, Editorial Director
Marc Sapir, Production Director
Curtis R. Scott, Associate Publisher

Edited by Emily Hall
Designed by Kimi Weart
Production by Matthew Pimm
Printed and bound by Ofset Yapimevi, Istanbul

This book is typeset in New Century Schoolbook,
Futura Bold, and Gilles' Comic Font.
The paper is 150gsm Amber Graphic.

Children's Book Working Group: Naomi Falk,
Samantha Friedman, Cari Frisch, Sophie Golub,
Emily Hall, Hannah Kim, Elizabeth Margulies,
Don McMahon, Matthew Pimm, Marc Sapir,
Curtis R. Scott, and Amanda Washburn

*With thanks to Paul Galloway, Andrew Gardner,
and Juliet Kinchin*

Library of Congress Control Number: 2021939681
ISBN: 978-1-63345-131-5

Published by The Museum of Modern Art
11 West 53 Street
New York, New York 10019
www.moma.org

Distributed in the United States and Canada
by Abrams Books for Young Readers, an imprint
of ABRAMS, New York
www.abramsbooks.com

Distributed outside the United States and Canada
by Thames & Hudson, London
www.thamesandhudson.com

Printed in Turkey

Photographs by Paige Knight (Jeep, Smart Car); Erik Landsberg
(Smart Car); Jonathan Muzikar (Citroën DS, Cistalia, Porsche 911,
Jaguar, Cinquecento, Airstream, Volkswagen)

CARS! CARS! CARS!

by **Kimi Weart**

Featuring Cars from the Collection of The Museum of Modern Art

The Museum of Modern Art, New York

Hello! My name is Rosario Abigail Bergen Delgado.
And I love cars. I *really* love cars.

All my toys are cars. I only draw cars.
I know everything there is to know about cars.
I can't wait until I can drive a car.

I asked my parents if I could drive the car.
I showed them how helpful I could be if they let me drive.

They said no.

So I dream about the day I will have my very own car.

Maybe it will be a race car. I would beat all the world records. And just think how fast I could get groceries home.

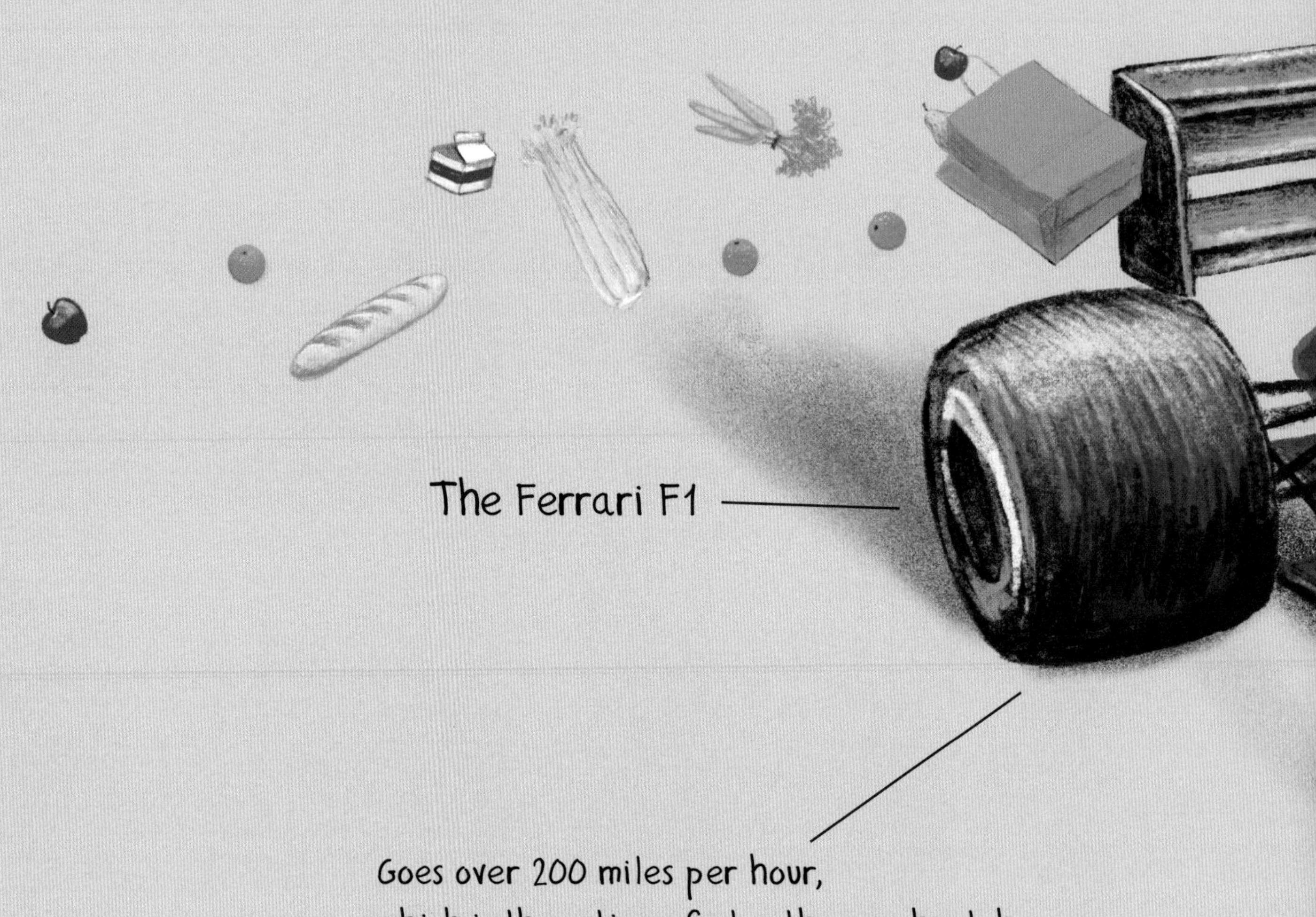

(Not actually good for getting groceries)

Or I might be an explorer.
An explorer needs a car that is big and tough,
so it can drive on the squashiest mud,
the bumpiest ground, the iciest ice.

Can carry up to 1,200 pounds,
which is like three baby elephants

Has open sides for quick escape, which is helpful if you get chased by baby elephants
The Jeep

If I wanted to visit the city
I would use this teeny-tiny car.
I would always find a parking spot.
Everyone else would be jealous.

The Smart Car
Can fit practically anywhere
Has room for a friend
Did I mention it can fit practically anywhere?

But that car has room for only one friend.
Maybe my car should have room for more friends.

Which is right for me?
A fast car?
A tough car?
A little car?
A big car?

Hmmm. This is hard.

I could be a super-cool secret agent and drive a super-cool car.

Or maybe it should be this one. Nobody would catch me.

Oooh, but what about this one?
It looks fast. When I put the top down
I would feel the wind in my hair.

I can't decide! What's a secret agent to do?

I haven't even chosen a color.
And I have so many favorite colors!

Big enough to bring four people to band practice, as long as no one plays the tuba

I love this trailer, too.
I would travel across the whole country, anywhere I wanted, and never have to leave home behind.

Called the Airstream because it cruises along like (can you guess?) a stream of air

The Grand Canyon

Called the Grand Canyon because it is simply grand

Before they invented cars
you couldn't just go wherever you wanted.
You traveled in a carriage pulled by horses
(or just walked)
on roads that mostly looked like this:

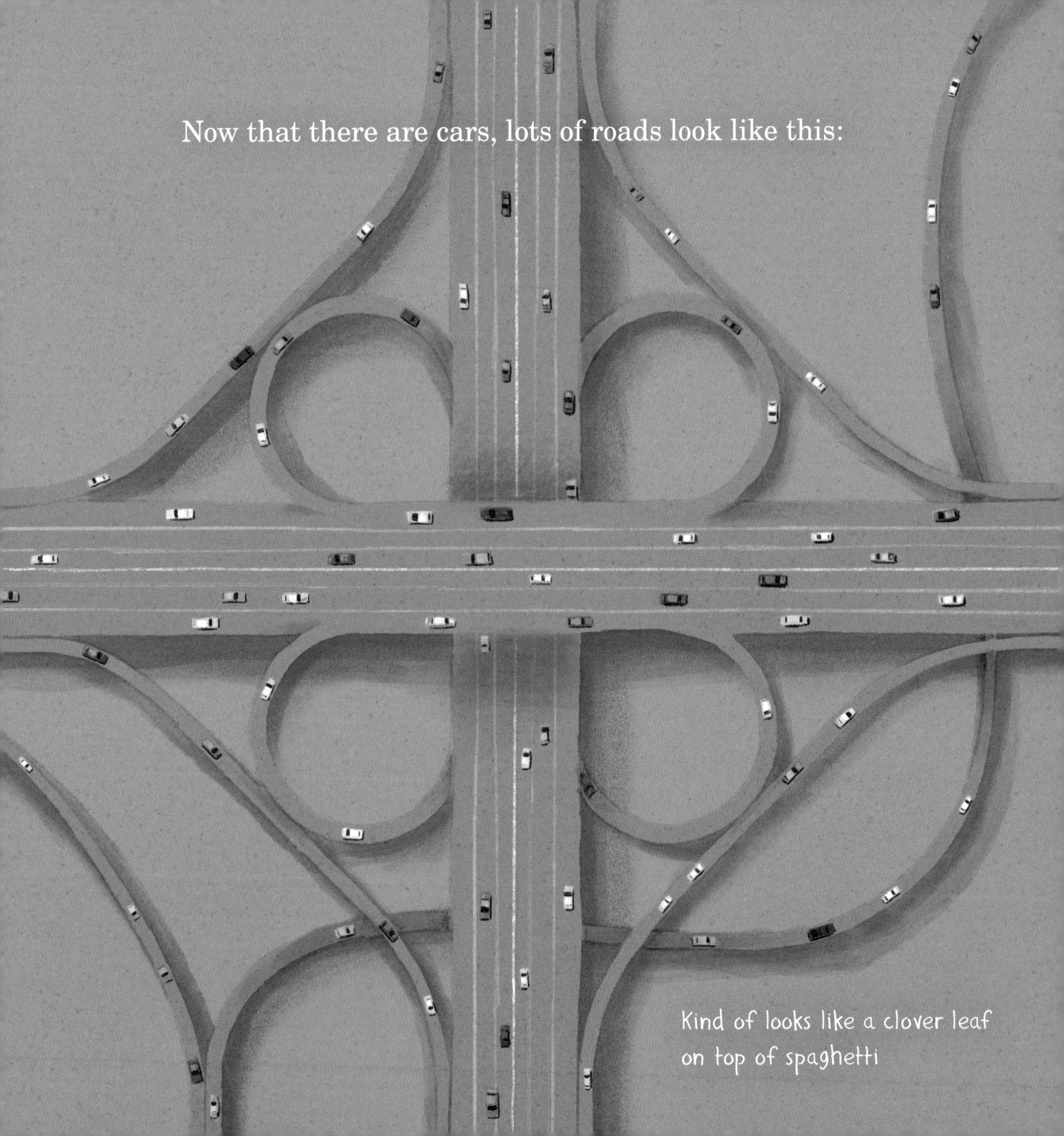
Now that there are cars, lots of roads look like this:
Kind of looks like a clover leaf
on top of spaghetti

Think about how cars have changed the world.
People have cut through mountains.

Built roads across deserts . . .

. . . and bridges that reach into the sky.

You can go anywhere and do anything
when you have a car.

One problem with cars is that most of them use gas. LOTS of gas. Using gas pollutes the air, which hurts the planet and all of us on it.

But this one doesn't need too much gas—and look how cute it is! Could this be the car for me?

The Volkswagen
(which in German means "people's car")

Most popular car ever—
more than 21 million sold!

Nicknamed "The Beetle"

See? Really does look like a bug

Wait—I have a better idea!
I will make a car that uses NO gas.
It will use batteries. And sunlight.
And wind power. And pedals.

WIND

I will make a little one.
A big one.
A fast one.
A tough one.
One that can go on water.
One that can fly!

I will make all kinds of cars.
MILLIONS of them!

But . . .

Then everyone would want one.
Maybe even *more* than one.
They would want to drive
a big car and a fast car
and a spy car and a purple, green, or blue car.
A car that can go on water
and a car that can fly.
The world would be covered in cars.
We would be up to our *eyeballs* in cars.

What if . . .

What if I got a bus?
A bus has room for ALL my friends.
A bus is better for the planet.
People can relax on a bus
and make friends on a bus.
They can chat and laugh and dream on a bus.
Just think how helpful I could be
if I had a bus . . .

Yes.

I should definitely get a bus.

Meet the Cars in the Collection of The Museum of Modern Art

The Museum of Modern Art was the first museum to draw attention to cars not just as useful machines but as true works of art—the catalogue for the 1951 exhibition *8 Automobiles* dubbed them “hollow, rolling sculptures.” In 1972 the first car was added to MoMA’s permanent collection: the gorgeous and extremely rare Cisitalia (only 170 were ever made). The collection has grown ever since.

Cars are symbols of power, freedom, and luxury, but they must also be recognized as a danger to the planet. Their emissions are one of the leading causes of global warming; they create toxic pollution that shortens life spans; and making a new car (even an electric car) depletes natural resources.

Engineers and designers are working to forge a better car for a cleaner future. One day cars will be so advanced that the ones we now see cruising along our streets and highways will look as ridiculous and old-fashioned as the rotary telephone. Children may one day look at the cars in this book and ask, “What’s that?”

This is why MoMA’s collection becomes even more important. The history of the car is one of innovation and artistic achievement. These objects of power and beauty, these rolling sculptures, deserve a spotlight in a museum of art.

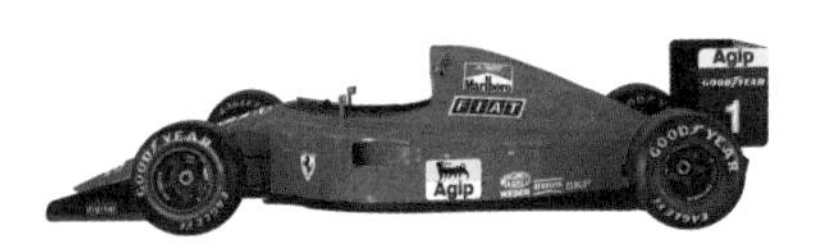

Ferrari Formula 1 racing car 641/2
Designed 1990 (this example 1990)
Designer: John Barnard
Manufacturer: Ferrari SpA, Maranello, Italy
Gift of the manufacturer

Jeep M38A1 utility truck
Designed 1952 (this example 1953)
Manufacturer: Willys-Overland Motors, Inc., Toledo, Ohio
Gift of DaimlerChrysler Corporation Fund

Smart Car coupé
Designed 1998 (this example 2002)
Manufacturer: Micro Compact Car Smart GmbH, Germany and France
Gift of the manufacturer, a company of the DaimlerChrysler Group

Citröen DS 23 sedan
Designed 1954–67 (this example 1973)
Designers: Flaminio Bertoni, Paul Magès, and Robert Opron
Manufacturer: Citröen, France
Gift of Christian Sumi, Zurich, and Sébastien and Pierre Nordenson

Cisitalia 202 GT car
Designed 1946 (this example 1948)
Designer: Pininfarina (Battista “Pinin” Farina)
Manufacturer: SpA Carrozzeria Pininfarina, Turin
Gift of the manufacturer

Porsche 911 coupé
Designed 1963 (this example 1965)
Designer: F. A. “Butzi” Porsche
Manufacturer: Porsche AG, Stuttgart
Gift of Thomas and Glwadys Seydoux

Jaguar E-Type roadster
Designed 1961 (this example 1963)
Designers: Sir William Lyons, Malcolm Sayer, and William M. Heynes
Manufacturer: Jaguar Ltd., Coventry, U.K.
Gift of Jaguar Cars

Fiat 500F city car (“Cinquecento”)
Designed 1957 (this example 1968)
Designer: Dante Giacosa
Manufacturer: Fiat SpA, Turin
Gift of Fiat Chrysler Automobiles Heritage

Airstream Bambi travel trailer
Designed 1960 (this example 1963)
Manufacturer: Airstream, Inc., Jackson Center, Ohio
Gift of Airstream, Inc.

Volkswagen Type 1 sedan
Designed 1938 (this example 1959)
Designer: Ferdinand Porsche
Manufacturer: Volkswagenwerk AG, Wolfsburg, Germany
Acquired with assistance from Volkswagen of America, Inc.
Conservation was made possible by a partnership with Volkswagen of America, Inc.

(p.s. The double-decker electric bus is made up, but I bet someone will make one soon)

Trustees of The Museum of Modern Art